PUFFIN B

KAMA VS YAMA

Dr Devdutt Pattanaik studied medicine but decided he loves telling stories better. He feels stories are like Eclair sweets; if you chew long enough, you get a burst of chocolate that is locked inside. So rather than working as a doctor, he decided to write and tell ancient Indian stories and reveal the idea-chocolate locked within them. He believes these stories are the gifts of our ancestors. He has been doing this for a long time and even uses the wisdom of these stories to help businesses. He is currently Chief Belief Officer of Future Group. To know more visit www.devdutt.com

Read these books in the *Fun in Devlok* series:

Indra Finds Happiness

An Identity Card for Krishna

Gauri and the Talking Cow

Saraswati's Secret River

Shiva Plays Dumb Charades

Kama
vs
Yama

—✳—

DEVDUTT PATTANAIK

Illustrations by Vishal Tondon

PUFFIN BOOKS

PUFFIN BOOKS

Published by the Penguin Group

Penguin Books India Pvt Ltd, 11 Community Centre, Panchsheel Park, New Delhi 110 017, India

Penguin Group (USA) Inc., 375 Hudson Street, New York, New York 10014, USA

Penguin Group (Canada), 90 Eglinton Avenue East, Suite 700, Toronto, Ontario, M4P 2Y3, Canada (a division of Pearson Penguin Canada Inc.)

Penguin Books Ltd, 80 Strand, London WC2R 0RL, England

Penguin Ireland, 25 St Stephen's Green, Dublin 2, Ireland (a division of Penguin Books Ltd)

Penguin Group (Australia), 250 Camberwell Road, Camberwell, Victoria 3124, Australia (a division of Pearson Australia Group Pty Ltd)

Penguin Group (NZ), 67 Apollo Drive, Rosedale, North Shore 0632, New Zealand (a division of Pearson New Zealand Ltd

Penguin Group (South Africa) (Pty) Ltd, 24 Sturdee Avenue, Rosebank, Johannesburg 2196, South Africa

Penguin Books Ltd, Registered Offices: 80 Strand, London WC2R 0RL, England

First published in Puffin by Penguin Books India 2011

Copyright © Devdutt Pattanaik 2011

ISBN 9780143331957

Typeset in Cochin by Abha Graphics
Printed at Manipal Press Ltd, Manipal

The stories in this series are inspired by various details of Hindu mythology and do not seek to supplement or substitute the original works.

You would not recognize him if you saw him. But perhaps, you would not see him at all. Most people would not. Long ago, he had been cursed: 'You shall lose your body and become invisible.'

But on one sunny day, he became visible to a little girl called Jayshree. Of course, when Jayshree saw him she did not recognize him. It had been a long time since anyone had seen him.

Jayshree was a strange little girl. She loved doing homework! As soon as she got home from school, she would wash her face and hands and feet, change her clothes, have her lunch and then sit down to do her homework. She would make a list of things to do, then do them, then revise what she had done, revise them again, and finally pack her bags for the next day.

When she slept, she dreamt about what homework she would be given the following day.

'Come, watch TV with us,' her father would say.

And Jayshree would reply, 'No, Daddy. I have homework to do.'

'Go out and play,' her mother would say.

And Jayshree would reply (you guessed it), 'No, Mummy, I have homework to do.'

But on that sunny day, Jayshree had this mysterious desire not to do

homework. She just wanted to lie down on her bed, watch television and eat potato chips. Never ever had Jayshree experienced such a desire! She wanted to put her pen down, shut her notebooks, munch on chips and watch some silly cartoon. The idea made her smile.

Should I do this or should I do that? Homework or chips? As she was thinking, she heard a commotion in the garden. It was on the far side, so she could not see who it was despite stretching her neck through her window. When the commotion continued, she went out to check who it was.

'Who is there?' Jayshree shouted.

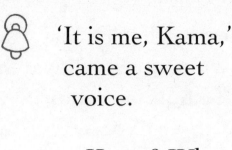

'It is me, Kama,' came a sweet voice.

Kama? Who Kama? Jayshree stepped out and saw a very handsome man in the garden. He was wearing bright robes that changed colour every time he moved. He was admiring the lotus buds in the lotus pond in the middle of the garden. 'Excuse me, who are you?'

Kama vs Yama

'You can see me? You can really see me? I don't believe it! This must be my lucky day!' said the man in the colourful robe.

Jayshree saw that he held a cane of sugar in his hand. It was a tall purple staff with green leaves on the top. It waved with the wind. Around it were a few honey bees. Strange, Jayshree thought. Who was this man?

'Of course I can see you. Why should I not?' asked Jayshree.

'Because I have been cursed that I shall lose my body and stay invisible. For thousands of years I have wandered this world invisible with my sugar cane bow. And now you can see me. This is a miracle. You must be a special child. What is your name?'

'Jayshree,' said Jayshree, wondering if she should call her mother. Kama seemed harmless and was extremely charming but he was a stranger nevertheless. And what was he doing in their garden with a shaft of sugar cane?

'You can call your mother but she will not see

me,' said Kama. 'No one can. I am surprised that you can see me.'

'You can read my thoughts!' Jayshree was alarmed and a little scared.

'I am a god, silly girl. Don't they teach you anything in school? Look at my feet; they don't touch the ground. And look carefully, I don't blink. And I don't sweat. What is the use of all that homework that you so love to do?' Jayshree did not know how to react. 'Oh, don't think so much, girl. Let us play. It has been ages since a human saw me. It feels good. Let us celebrate this moment. Let us play. Or would you rather watch television and eat chips? I love chips too.'

Suddenly hundreds of butterflies
entered the garden. They danced
around Kama's head. Kama spread
out his hand and walked around
the garden. And in every direction

he went, tender shoots of grass burst forth from the ground and trees exploded to release flowers of all colours. Every flower released the sweetest of perfumes in the air. Golden nectar enclosed by their petals glittered in the sunlight. Dozens of parrots descended from the sky. They had bright red beaks and bright green feathers. They sat on Kama's shoulders and flapped their wings as if to welcome an old friend.

Jayshree was overwhelmed by the heady scent and the bright colours around her. She forgot all about her homework!

'That is what this idiot does. Makes you forget homework and all the

important things you are supposed to do,' boomed a voice.

Jayshree turned and saw a black buffalo right behind her, chewing the grass thoughtfully and looking at her as if she was a criminal. Jayshree felt guilty and shameful. She did not know why.

On top of this buffalo was a stern looking man. He wore dull grey robes that were crumpled and his lips looked as if they had never curved to smile and he had a big thick and very long moustache.

In his hand he held a diary. 'I can see,' said the man, referring to his diary, 'that you have just finished your English homework. There is still Math

and Science waiting to be done. And
you have to cover your Geography
book with brown paper. The old cover
is damaged because of the ink you
spilled on it. And your pencils need to
be sharpened for the drawing exam
tomorrow.'

'How do you know these things?'

'Because I am supposed to know everything that everyone is supposed to do. I am Yama,' said the man matter-of-factly.

'Ignore him, Jayshree,' said Kama. 'He is no fun.'

'She cannot
ignore me.
No one can.
I follow
everyone
everywhere.
People just
don't see me,'
said the man on
the buffalo.

'Because no one *wants*
to see you,' sneered
Kama.

'And no one *can* see
you,' retorted Yama.

'Leave this girl alone. She can see me.
I finally have a friend. And we want to

play or watch television or eat chips.
You are not invited,' shouted Kama.

'I don't need invitations. I will not
leave her. She has homework to do.
And having you around is not helping
her. You will make her forget her
responsibilities. You are no friend,'
said Yama, sounding rather superior.

Jayshree did not like Yama. But he did
speak the truth. She had homework
to do, but she was enjoying herself in
the garden. She had never seen such
flowers or smelt such perfumes and
she could not take her eyes off the
butterflies and parrots. Oh, what was
she to do?

'Let us go shopping,' said Kama. 'Let

me buy you a bright new dress. Your clothes look so boring.' Jayshree jumped up excited. 'We can travel on my parrot.'

'See how he distracts you, Jayshree,' said Yama. 'That is what he does. That is why he was cursed to become invisible.'

Jayshree wanted to know more. So Yama told the story of how Kama came to be cursed.

Long ago, there was a young boy called Shekchilli. His father gave him a pot of milk to go and sell in the market. On the way, Shekchilli began to think. 'If I sell this milk, I will get some money. I will not give all the money to my father. I will keep a coin for myself. Tomorrow, Father will give me another pot of milk to sell. Again, I will not give him all the money. I will keep a coin for myself. In this way, I will collect many coins. When I have enough, I will buy a goat. The goat will give milk. I will sell the milk and make more money. The goat will have children. Some I will sell and some I will keep so that even they give me milk. All that milk I will sell and make a lot of money. I will use that money to buy a cow. The cow will give more milk and I will sell it to earn more money. When I have a lot of money, I

will buy a house. When I buy a house, I will get a wife. And my wife will cook food for me. And she will keep nagging me to come and eat. And I will shake my head and say, later, I will eat later, not now as I have work to do.' As Shekchilli kept daydreaming like this, he did not see a rock on the road. He stumbled

Kama vs Yama

on it and fell flat on the ground. The pot of milk on his head broke and all the milk was spilled. He was so angry that he cursed Kama, the god who makes you dream, to turn invisible.

'Hey, that is not correct,' said Kama. 'Shekchilli did not curse me.'

'Then who cursed you?' asked Jayshree.

'It was Shiva.'

Kama then told the story of how Shiva cursed him.

Shiva was a hermit who lived on Mount Kailash, which is covered with snow all year round. He wanted everyone to leave him alone. He was happy all by himself. He certainly did not want to marry. But Parvati, the princess of the mountains, wanted to marry him. She would travel to Mount Kailash every day and offer him fruits and flowers. Shiva would show no interest. He would keep his eyes firmly shut and not even bother to smile at the poor princess. Kama felt sorry for the princess and decided to help her. So he mounted his parrot and flew down to Mount Kailash. He picked up a flower and turned it into an arrow. He turned his shaft of sugar cane into a bow and requested the honey bees to fly in single line and serve as the bowstring. Thus he created a very special weapon that can make a man fall in love with a woman. Kama raised

the love bow
and shot the love
arrow at Shiva.
When Shiva was
shot at by the love
arrow he opened
his eyes and fell in
love with Parvati.
But something else
happened.
A third eye
appeared
on his
forehead
and out
came a
missile
of fire and its flames engulfed Kama.
And before Kama could say anything,
his body had been reduced to ashes.

Parvati was horrified. She begged
Shiva not to be so angry because
Kama was only trying to help. So
Shiva said, 'Kama will not die but he
will lose his body and stay invisible.'

'And did Shiva and Parvati marry?'
asked Jayshree.

'Of course they did. My arrows
never fail,' said Kama with a cheeky
smile. 'I even shot one at you so that you
stopped thinking of homework
and started thinking about television
and chips.'

'Aha, so you distracted me. You
made me dream. Turned me into a
Shekchilli.' Jayshree suddenly did
not like Kama as she did before.

'I told you that is what he does,'
said Yama.

Kama defended himself. 'If you do
only what is written in Yama's diary,
life will be boring. Imagine, if I had
not shot my arrow, Shiva would
have never opened his eyes and
Parvati, the poor princess of the
mountains, would have never got
married.'

'Nonsense. They were supposed to
marry. My diary said so. You should
not have interfered, ' said Yama. Yama's
buffalo nodded his head vigorously.

'If Yama had his way, everyone in
this world would be like Gangu Teli,'
said Kama.

'Who is Gangu Teli?' asked Jayshree.

Kama told her about Gangu Teli.
Gangu was a Teli, meaning a man who
makes oil. He had to press a bag full
of oilseeds in an oil-presser all day to

get one or two pots of oil. Pressing oil is a boring task. One has to go around rotating the presser all day. One can do nothing else all day. Just go round and round and round. No fun, just work and work and work.

'That is what Yama will make you—a Gangu Teli, pressing oil from oilseeds all day,' said Kama.

'I don't make oil,' clarified Jayshree.

'Oh, but you do homework. And you don't play and you don't have fun. Even your parents find you boring. Boring like Yama, just doing tasks and following his diary and never enjoying himself. You are no different from poor Gangu Teli.'

Yama defended himself. 'If Gangu Teli did not do what he was supposed to do, and spent his time daydreaming like Shekchilli, no one would get oil. What use is fun? It is just a waste of time. I feel every minute should be spent doing some work that helps the world. There is so much to do.'

Jayshree remembered something. She said, 'All work and no play makes Jack a dull boy. Gangu Teli is Jack.'

'Yes,' said Kama, glad that he had convinced Jayshree.

Yama retorted, 'All play and no work also make Jack a dull boy. Shekchilli is also Jack.'

Jayshree said, 'I don't want to be Shekchilli and I don't want to be Gangu Teli. I don't want to be either.'

'Then you will be Mitti ka Madho,' said both Yama and Kama. 'Or Gobar ki Gani.' They proceeded to explain what these two phrases meant.

Mitti means mud and Gobar means cowdung. A farmer was very unhappy because his children never listened to him. They never talked to him, and they never obeyed him. Frustrated, the farmer and his wife went to the temple and sought the help of the gods.

The farmer went to the Krishna temple and asked Krishna to give him a child who would always obey him.

The farmer's wife went to the Ganesha temple and also asked for a child who would always obey the farmer.

Krishna took some mud and created out of it a boy whose name was Mitti ka Madho. Ganesha took some cowdung and created out of a

girl called Gobar ki Gani. 'Here you are,' said Krishna and Ganesha. 'Two children who will do nothing else but what you tell them to do.'

The farmer and his wife returned home with the boy and the girl, very happy to have two obedient children. But soon they realized that the children did nothing else but obey them. If they told the children to 'stand up', they stood up. If they told the children to 'sit down', they sat down. They never did anything on their own.

Once the farmer's wife told Mitti ka Madho, 'Go to the market and buy some sugar.' Madho went to the

market and bought sugar but did not
return home. He kept waiting in the
market because his mother had not
told him to return home.

Another time the farmer told Gobar ki
Gani, 'Go take a bath.' Gani took a bath
but did not step out of the bathroom
because her father had not told her so.

'Such stupid silly kids,' said Jayshree.
'They are useless!'

'The two children are neither
Shekchilli nor Gangu Teli,' said Yama.

'You must be either Shekchilli or
Gangu Teli,' said Kama.

'Choose my way—do what you are

supposed to do. Do your duties!'
said Yama.

'Choose my way—do what you feel
like. Have fun!' said Kama.

Jayshree did not know whom to
choose. She loved doing homework.
But sometimes she loved eating chips
and watching television too.

She looked at Kama. He was so cute
and charming with his colourful
clothes, his sugar cane, his parrots,
his bees and butterflies. He made her
feel so happy and carefree. But he
was so irresponsible. He did not care
that his arrow caused Shekchilli to
daydream and fall and break his pot
and lose all his milk. Jayshree was

not sure if she liked Kama.

Jayshree then looked at Yama. He looked so stern with his dull clothes and his buffalo and his diary. And he was so strict about doing one's tasks.

Kama whispered in Jayshree's ears, 'Yama is the god of death. Surely, you know. If you choose him, he will kill you.'

Yama overheard Kama because his ears are very sharp. He said, 'Being the god of death is not a bad thing at all. When you have done all that you are supposed to do as per my diary, you must leave the earth. It is my job to help you leave the earth.'

'And where do we go?' asked Jayshree

'Across the river Vaitarni to the land of the dead,' answered Yama.

'And if I did not exist,' said Kama, 'everyone would stay in the land of dead. I bring people back into the land of the living.'

'Are you saying that I was once in the land of the dead? How come I don't remember?' asked Jayshree.

'The river Vaitarni takes
away all memories,'
said Yama. 'If I did
not exist, all things
would stay on earth and
the earth would become
a very crowded place.'

Jayshree looked at the garden, the
trees, the flowers, the lotus pond
and realized how beautiful it was,
thanks to Kama. But if Yama did not
exist, the flowers and the butterflies
would stay in the garden forever.
They would never go. Things would
get boring.

'I am Sunday and all holidays,' said
Kama. 'A day without rules and all fun.'
'I am Monday and all workdays,'

said Yama. 'A day with rules and tasks to do.'

Both were trying hard to make her choose one or the other.

'Can I choose both of you? I love Kama but I also like Yama. I like doing homework but sometimes I would like to watch television and eat chips too,' said Jayshree.

'Of course you can,' said Kama.

'You will be like Raja Bhoj,' said Yama.

The gods then told Jayshree about Raja Bhoj. He was a wise king. For one half of the month, from new moon

Kama vs Yama

to full moon, when the moon would wax, he would sit in court, and do everything a ruler is supposed to do— building roads and solving problems and settling disputes. For the other half of the month, from full moon to new moon, when the moon wanes, he would spend time playing with his wife and children, listening to music and watching dance performances, swimming in the river or riding on elephants in the forest.

'He balanced Kama and Yama,' exclaimed Jayshree. 'Yes, I want to be Raja Bhoj.'

'So you will be,' said the two gods.

Kama then rose to the sky on his

parrot, waved his sugar cane and flew
towards the east. Yama nodded his
head, tapped his diary and got on to
his buffalo to walk towards the west.

Jayshree found herself all alone in
the garden.

She took a decision. 'First I will finish
my homework. Then I will watch
television and eat chips.' It felt good to
be Raja Bhoj.